P9-CQW-699

DOVER · THRIFT · EDITIONS

Oedipus at Colonus

SOPHOCLES

DOVER PUBLICATIONS, INC.
Mineola, New York

DOVER THRIFT EDITIONS

GENERAL EDITOR: PAUL NEGRI

EDITOR OF THIS VOLUME: JULIE NORD

Copyright

Theatrical Rights

This Dover Thrift Edition may be used in its entirety, in adaptation, or in any other way for theatrical productions, professional and amateur, in the United States, without permission, fee, or acknowledgment. (This may not apply outside of the United States, as copyright conditions may vary.)

Bibliographical Note

This Dover edition, first published in 1999, is an unabridged republication of the play *Oedipus Coloneus* from the volume *The Dramas of Sophocles Rendered in English Verse Dramatic & Lyric by Sir George Young*, as published by J. M. Dent & Sons, Ltd., London, in 1906. (The Dent edition was the second, the first having been published by George Bell & Sons, London, in 1888.) See the new Note, specially written for the Dover edition, for further details.

Library of Congress Cataloging-in-Publication Data

Sophocles.
   [Oedipus at Colonus. English]
   Oedipus at Colonus / Sophocles.
      p.   cm. — (Dover thrift editions)
   "This Dover edition . . . is an unabridged republication of the play . . . from the volume *The Dramas of Sophocles Rendered in English Verse Dramatic & Lyric by Sir George Young*, as published by J. M. Dent & Sons, Ltd., London, in 1906."
   ISBN 0-486-40659-8 (pbk.)
   1. Oedipus (Greek mythology)—Drama. I. Young, George, Sir, 1837–1930. II. Title. III. Series.
PA4414.O5Y68   1999
882'.01—dc21
                                                 99-21444
                                                 CIP

Manufactured in the United States of America
Dover Publications, Inc., 31 East 2nd Street, Mineola, N.Y. 11501

Note

SOPHOCLES (born ca. 496 B.C., died after 413) was one of the three major authors of Greek tragedy. He wrote some 123 plays, only seven of which survive in full. These works brought him extraordinary acclaim in his day, for in the annual Dionysian festival they never won less than second place, and they captured first place twenty times. *Oedipus at Colonus* was, as far as we know, the last play Sophocles wrote; it was first produced, by his son, several years following his death.

Although relatively little is known of Sophocles' life, we do know that he was born in Colonus and was a prominent citizen of Athens for most of his long life. There is a special poignancy, then, to this play. It paints a restrained but heartfelt portrait of Athens, its people and its ruler, who, despite initial misgivings, show great fair-mindedness, integrity, and empathy in their dealings with the figure of Oedipus—a forbidding and difficult presence, at best, in this drama. This portrait may well have represented Sophocles' last public tribute to the city, the civilization, to which he was so dedicated. In addition, the play's setting, Colonus—the spot where Oedipus' sufferings will come to an end, where he is to willingly obey the will of the gods, and the spot which the oracles have told him will be protected henceforth, once he chooses it for his burial ground—may well capture the great tragedian's own wish to bestow a final blessing on his birthplace.

The three plays that are sometimes called the Theban or Cadmean Trilogy were written over a forty-year period and not in order of dramatic chronology: *Oedipus the King, Oedipus at Colonus, Antigone.* They also contradict each other frequently. It has been noted, for instance, that the character of Creon is wildly different from play to play; that circumstances presented at the close of *Oedipus the King* are overlooked or radically changed at the outset of *Oedipus at Colonus,* and so on. Therefore, although it is quite possible to learn interesting things by comparing them, it is widely agreed that the three should be considered separate dramatic entities.

The translation by Sir George Young (1837–1930) reprinted here is not only very accurate; it also preserves the feeling of the original Greek to a great extent. The verse forms are reasonable English equivalents; the diction—lightly archaic in the blank-verse dialogues, heightened and more complex in the stanzaic choruses—admirably reflects the hieratic nature of Sophocles' drama.

In the present edition, Sir George's own notes (exclusively concerned with problems of the Greek text and its interpretation) have been omitted. Several new, very brief footnotes have been added, identifying references to places or deities with which the reader may not be familiar; when they may be found in standard reference works, unfamiliar references have not been footnoted.

Persons Represented

ŒDIPUS.

ANTIGONE,
ISMENE, } *his daughters.*

THESEUS, *king of Athens.*

CREON.

POLYNICES, *son to Œdipus.*

A Stranger, *an inhabitant of Colonus.*

A Messenger, *an Athenian attending on Theseus.*

The CHORUS *is composed of citizens of Colonus.*
Guards attending on Theseus and Creon.
An attendant following Ismene.

Oedipus at Colonus

Oedipus at Colonus

Scene—Colonus, before the Sacred Grove of the Erinyes.

[*Enter* ŒDIPUS *and* ANTIGONE.]

ŒDIPUS   Antigone, child of a blind old man,
What lands are these, or what the folk whose gates
We have attained? Who shall receive to-day
With stinted alms the wanderer Œdipus?—
Asking but little; than that little still
Obtaining less; and yet enough for me.
For my afflictions and the weight of years
And something, too, of my own dignity
Teach me contentment. If you see, my child,
Some resting-place, either by sacred grove
Or secular dwelling, stay me and set me down,
That we may find out in what place we are;
For strangers from inhabitants to learn
We are come hither; and what we hear, to do it.
ANTIGONE   Towers are there, O my father, Œdipus,
Covering a city, I perceive, afar;
This place, as I suppose, is consecrate;
It blooms with laurel, olive and the vine;[1]
Thick-flying nightingales within it warble;
Here stretch thy limbs, upon this rough-hewn stone;
For thou art aged to have come so far.

[1]The laurel is sacred to Apollo, the olive to Athena, and the vine to Dionysus. The presence of these things therefore demonstrates the sacred nature of the spot. Nightingales may have indicated, in addition, the presence of Pan.

ŒDIPUS   Seat me and guard me still; for I am blind.
ANTIGONE   I know—that is an old tale—tell not me.
ŒDIPUS   Well, can you teach me whither we are come?
ANTIGONE   To Athens, that I know; but not the quarter.
ŒDIPUS   So much we heard from every passenger.
ANTIGONE   But shall I go and ask what place it is?
ŒDIPUS   Why yes, my child; if it seems hospitable.
ANTIGONE   O yes, there are some dwellings.—There's no need,
        I think: for here's a man, I see, close to us.
ŒDIPUS   What, moving and approaching hitherward?
ANTIGONE   Yes, here, I mean, at hand. Say what is needful;
        This is the man.

[*Enter a Stranger, an inhabitant of Colonus.*]

ŒDIPUS   Stranger, this maiden tells me
        (Whose eyesight serves both for herself and me)
        Of your approach, an apt intelligencer
        Of things we cannot guess—
STRANGER   Ere you ask further
        Come from that seat; you trespass on a place
        No foot may desecrate.
ŒDIPUS   What is the place?
        To what God dedicated?
STRANGER   It is kept
        From touch or dwelling: the dread Goddesses
        Hold it, the daughters of the Earth and Gloom.
ŒDIPUS   Who? By what solemn name denominate
        Might I invoke them?
STRANGER   By the natives here
        They would be called the All-seeing Favourers;
        Other fit names elsewhere.
ŒDIPUS   May they receive
        With mercy me their supplicant; and I
        From this land's harbour will go forth no more!
STRANGER   What does this mean?
ŒDIPUS   'Tis my misfortunes' weird.
STRANGER   Truly I dare not turn him out, before
        I tell the rest—without authority.
ŒDIPUS   Sir, in Heaven's name do not begrudge me—me
        A wanderer—what I crave of you to say!
STRANGER   Explain, and I will show I grudge you not.
ŒDIPUS   What ground is this we have been treading on?

STRANGER   You shall hear all I know. First the whole place is holy,
Inhabited by dread Poseidon;[2] next
The Deity that brought fire abides in it,
Titan Prometheus;[3] this same spot you press
They call the Brass-paved Causeway[4] of the land—
Rampart of Athens; the adjoining farms
Boast them Colonus[5] mounted on his horse
For their chief patron, and the people all
Are called by and in common bear his name.
These are the facts, sir stranger; honoured not
So much in story, as cherished on the spot.

ŒDIPUS   Did you say any men lived hereabouts?

STRANGER   Yes truly, and that they bear this Hero's name.

ŒDIPUS   Have they a chief, or lies it with the folk
To hold debate?

STRANGER   These parts are in the rule
Of the king of the City.

ŒDIPUS   Who is he whose might
And counsel sway them?

STRANGER   Theseus is his name,
Old Ægeus' son.

ŒDIPUS   Would one of you go fetch him?

STRANGER   What should one tell or move him to come here for?

ŒDIPUS   Say, to gain much by a small act of kindness.

STRANGER   And where's the service in a man that's blind?

ŒDIPUS   There will be eyes in all that I shall say.

STRANGER   Come, this you may, sir, and without offence;
(Since you are worshipful to look upon,
Saving God's hand;) stay there where I first found you,
While I go tell this to the burghers round,
(Here, not in the city;) they will soon decide
If you shall tarry, or depart once more.   [*Exit.*

ŒDIPUS   My daughter, has the stranger gone away?

ANTIGONE   Yes, he has gone. You may say anything
Securely, father; none are here but I.

ŒDIPUS   Queens, with stern faces! since of all this land
First in your sanctuary I seated me,

---

[2]*Poseidon*] God of the sea.

[3]*Prometheus*] The god who gave fire to humankind; he was punished by Zeus but the
Greeks considered him to be perhaps their greatest ally amongst the gods.

[4]*Brass-paved Causeway*] The dread pathway to Hades (elsewhere called the "Brazen
stairs").

[5]*Colonus*] Nothing is known of this hero, for whom the town is named.

To Phœbus,[6] as to me, turn no deaf ear,
Who, prophesying of those my many woes,
Spake of this respite for me at the last
That when my journey ended, in a land
Where I should find asylum, at the shrine
Of awful Powers, and hospitality,
There I should round the goal of my life-sorrow,
There dwell, a blessing to my hosts—a curse
To those who sent me into banishment;
Giving me rede a sign of this should come,
In earthquake, thunder, or lightning out of heaven.
Now I perceive it is from none but you,
The faithful omen that has guided me
Along my pathway hither to this grove.
Else I should never in my wayfaring
Have met you first so fitly—strangers you
To wine,[7] as I am—or have taken seat
Upon this awful footstone, all unhewn.
Now therefore, Goddesses, bestow on me,
According to Apollo's oracle,
Some passing, some quick finish of my life;
If I appear not still unperfected
In my continual servitude of toils,
The extremest mortals know. Come, you kind daughters
Of ancient Gloom! Come, thou that bear'st the name
Of mightiest Pallas,[8] Athens, first of cities,
Have pity upon this miserable ghost
Of what was Œdipus! He is not now
Such as of old.

ANTIGONE   Hush! there are people coming,
Elders in years, who note you where you sit.

ŒDIPUS   I will be silent, and do you conceal me
Apart within the grove, till I may learn
What language these men hold; for in the knowledge
Prudence consists for what we have to do.

[ŒDIPUS *and* ANTIGONE *retire.*

[*Enter Citizens of Colonus, as Chorus.*]

---

[6]*Phoebus*] Apollo, god of light and truth. It was his oracle (at Delphi) that prophesied Oedipus' crimes and subsequent fate.
[7]*strangers you to wine*] It was forbidden to pour wine as libation to the Eumenides, the "Queens, with stern faces" to whom Oedipus speaks.
[8]*Pallas*] Athena, goddess of wisdom.

Chorus

Look! Who was it? Where abides he?
In what nook or corner hides he—
Of all men—of all mankind the most presuming?
  Search about. Spy him, there!
  Seek him out everywhere.
A vagrant—some vagrant the grey-beard must have been
   None of our countrymen.
Otherwise he never would have dreamt of coming
To the untrodden thicket of the Virgins here,
Of the mighty Powers, whom to name we fear,
  Whose abode we pass unprying,
  Without babble or loud crying,
   Keeping mouth closely pent
   Save on what is innocent.
   Now, 'tis said, void of dread,
Some one has intruded on the sacred space;
   I the bound searching round
Cannot yet alight upon his hiding place.

ŒDIPUS   [*advancing, with* ANTIGONE] I am the man; for by the sound
   I see you,
 As is the saying.
1 CITIZEN   Hilloa! hoa! who is this,
 Dreadful to see, dreadful to hear?
ŒDIPUS   I pray you,
 Do not regard me as a trespasser—
1 CITIZEN   Averting Jove! who may this old man be?
ŒDIPUS   One of a sort far other than the first
 To be deemed happy, O you guardians
 Over this land; I am myself the proof;
 I should not otherwise be groping thus,
 Led by another's eyesight, or, being great,
 On slender moorings come to anchorage.

Chorus

Eh thine eyes! thy blind eyes!
Wert thou thus, as I surmise,
For sad life—for long life—equipped from life's beginning?
  None the more, if so be,
  Shalt thou score, spite of me,

On curses fresh curses, by sinning—yea, by sinning.
　　But that thou trespass not
On the grassy coverts of this hallowed spot,
Where the bowl of water by the herbage quaffed
Flows with mingled runnels of a sweetened draught—
　　Beware, beware sirrah stranger!
　　Get thee hence! Avoid thy danger!
　　(His long start costs me dear);
　　Thou tired vagabond, dost hear?
　　Though thou bring word or thing
Hither for debate, avoid the sacred glen!
　　Passing where all may fare
Speak with freedom; but refrain thee, until then!

ŒDIPUS　Daughter, what course is to be thought of, now?
ANTIGONE　My father, what the citizens observe
　　That should we also; yield in what we must,
　　And hearken.
ŒDIPUS　　　　　　Well, give me a hand.
ANTIGONE　　　　　　　　　　　　You have it.
ŒDIPUS　Sirs, let me meet no wrong, if I remove
　　Trusting in you.
CITIZEN　　　　　Never against thy will
　　Out of these sanctuaries, ancient sir,
　　Shall any drag thee.
ŒDIPUS　　　　　　Am I to proceed?
1 CITIZEN　Yes, further yet.
ŒDIPUS　　　　　　Still further?
1 CITIZEN　　　　　　　　　Damsel, lead,
　　And bring him further on; for you perceive.
ANTIGONE　Follow, my father, follow in my train,
　　With feet all darkling.
1 CITIZEN　　　　　　Man of woes, endure,
　　Being as thou art, a stranger on strange soil,
　　To abhor whate'er the City has held in hate,
　　And what She loves, to honour.
ŒDIPUS　　　　　　　　Come, my child,
　　Lead me where, stepping without sacrilege,
　　Something we may impart, something receive;
　　And let us not contend with fate.
1 CITIZEN　　　　　　　　Halt there!
　　No further bend thy steps, over that ramp
　　Of rock in front.

ŒDIPUS   What, thus?
1 CITIZEN   Yes, as you have it.
ŒDIPUS   May I be seated?
1 CITIZEN   Yes, if you bend sideways,
          And sit down low, just on the edge of the stone.
ANTIGONE   Father, this is my office; gently take
          One step with my step, and commit—
ŒDIPUS   Eh me!
ANTIGONE   Thine aged frame to loving hand of mine.
ŒDIPUS   [*seated*] Ah, my misfortune!
1 CITIZEN   Man of woes, declare
          (Now that thou art at ease) what was thy birth,
          What toil-worn wanderer thou art, what country
          We are to know for thine.
ŒDIPUS   Ah strangers,
          I am an outcast; but forbear, forbear—
1 CITIZEN   Why do you put this matter from you, sir?
ŒDIPUS   Forbear, I say, to ask me what I am,
          Nor seek nor question further.
1 CITIZEN   Wherefore so?
ŒDIPUS   Awful my birth.
1 CITIZEN   Tell it.
ŒDIPUS   O child—ah me,
          What must I answer?
1 CITIZEN   Of what seed thou art
          Of the father's side, sir, say.
ŒDIPUS   Woe's me, my child,
          What will become of me?
ANTIGONE   Speak, for you tread
          The very verge.
ŒDIPUS   I will; I have no refuge.
1 CITIZEN   Ye are both long about it; make more speed!
ŒDIPUS   Know ye of one from Laius—
1 CITIZEN   Ha, how? how?
ŒDIPUS   And of the race of Labdacus—
1 CITIZEN   O Jove!
ŒDIPUS   Miserable Œdipus?
1 CITIZEN   And art thou he?
ŒDIPUS   Have ye no fear at what I say—
CITIZENS   Oh! oh!
ŒDIPUS   Unhappy!
CITIZENS   Out, O out!

ŒDIPUS   Now, daughter,
        What must we look for next?
CITIZENS   Off, off,
        Out of the place!
ŒDIPUS   And what you promised me,
        What will you make of that?

Chorus

        No retribution hath Fortune in store
        For the man who requites what he suffered before;
        Treason, by treason withstood, and surpassed,
        Pays a man trouble, not favour, at last.
        Now back with you, back! You have sailing orders.
        Get out of this place! Go forth from our borders!
        Bring to our gates no more evil fates!
ANTIGONE   Pious strangers,
                Although you brook not
        The old man's presence, my father, here,
                To what he did
                (Though not with purpose)
        Listening, lending an open ear,
        Me, not the less, poor maid, I entreat,
        Pity, O strangers, who fall at your feet—
        Fall at your feet, for my father's sake only
            With eyes unblasted facing your face,
            Even as though born one of your race,
        So mercy may light on the helpless and lonely!
        On you, as on Heaven, we depend; reject not
        The prayer of the poor, for grace we expect not.
        By all you hold dear as your own heart's blood!
        By your brood! By your bed! By your need! By your God!
        You will find no man, searching with heed,
        But he must follow, if God lead.

1 CITIZEN   Daughter of Œdipus, both him and you,
            Trust us, we pity alike, in your distress;
            But, reverencing Heaven, we have no power
            To go beyond what has been told you now.
ŒDIPUS   What is the use of reputation, then,
            Or what of good report, flowing all to nothing,
            If it be said of Athens, that she is
            The most religious and the only state
            Able to guard the stranger in distress,

And that she only can suffice his need,
While you—to me—what have you done with it?
Who from these steps dislodged me, and then, in fear
Of my name, merely, are expelling me;
For of my person it is not, or my deeds;
The things I did were rather done to me—
If I must speak of that my parentage,
For which, as well I know, you are scared at me.
And after all, where was my villainy?
I but requited evil done to me;
So that, although I did it knowingly,
Not even then should I be proved a villain.
But as it is, I went the way I went
Unwittingly; and suffered at the hands
Of those who knew that they were injuring me.
Wherefore in Heaven's name I beseech you, sirs,
Even as you raised me from my seat, now save me,
And do not, in your reverence for Gods,
Make nought of the Gods' dues; rather consider
How that they mark the virtuous among men,
And mark the wicked too; and that escape
Was never yet, of any man profane.
In whose obedience tarnish not the fame
Of Athens the august, lending your hand
To any act of profanation. No!
As you received the suppliant, on your promise,
So rescue and preserve me; and survey
These brows, of ill aspect, not without honour.
For holy and righteous am I, who come hither,
And I bring profit to these citizens;
And when that lord arrives, who is your leader,
If you will hearken, I will tell you all;
In the mean time see that you deal not falsely.

1 CITIZEN   We needs must feel a certain awe, old man,
At that which you suggest; for it is couched
In words of no light weight. Sufficeth us
That the land's rulers should decide the case.

ŒDIPUS   And where is he who rules this country, sirs?

1 CITIZEN   He keeps his father's hold, here; but a post,
The same who sent me hither, is gone to fetch him.

ŒDIPUS   Do you suppose he will give heed, or take,
For a blind man, the trouble to draw near?

1 CITIZEN   Ay truly, when he hears your name.

ŒDIPUS   But who
    Is there to tell him that?
1 CITIZEN   'Tis a long way;
    But travellers' gossip often gets abroad,
    Which when he hears, he will come, never fear.
    For far and wide, old man, has your name travelled;
    So that, although he sleep, and tarry long,
    Hearing of you, he will make haste and come.
ŒDIPUS   I wish he may, for his own city's good
    And mine. For who does not befriend himself
    By doing good?
ANTIGONE   O Jove, what shall I say?
    What shall I think, my father?
ŒDIPUS   But what is it,
    Antigone, my child?
ANTIGONE   I see a woman
    Coming toward us, mounted on a horse
    Of Ætnean breed; and a Thessalian bonnet
    Is on her head, tied close about her face,
    To screen it from the sun. What shall I say?
    Is it—or not? or do my thoughts mislead?
    Yes! No! I know not what to say. Alack,
    It is no other. Yes, and she looks joyful
    At spying me, as she draws near, and shews
    It is no other than Ismene's self!
ŒDIPUS   How say you, child?
ANTIGONE   Why, that I see your child,
    My sister; you can tell her by the voice.

[Enter ISMENE *and attendant.]*

ISMENE   Father—and sister! the two names to me
    That are most dear! How hardly have I found you,
    And hardly can regard you now, for grief!
ŒDIPUS   O child, are you come hither?
ISMENE   O my father,
    Hapless to look on!
ŒDIPUS   Are you here, my child?
ISMENE   After much trouble, yes.
ŒDIPUS   Touch me, my girl.
ISMENE   I touch you, both of you.
ŒDIPUS   Offspring of mine—
    Sisters—

ISMENE   Alas, what miseries—
ŒDIPUS   Hers and mine?
ISMENE   Yes, and my own, wretch that I am!
ŒDIPUS   My child,
        Why did you come?
ISMENE   Father, in care for you.
ŒDIPUS   You wanted me?
ISMENE   ·   Yes, and to bring you news
        In person, with my one true servant here.
ŒDIPUS   And the young men your brothers, where have they
        Bestowed their labour?
ISMENE   They are—where they are;
        It is a heavy time with them, just now.
ŒDIPUS   O how exactly fitted are that pair,
        In character and training, for the ways
        Followed in Egypt! For the husbands there
        Sit within walls and weave, while out of doors
        Their partners fare, winning their daily food.
        Even so, my children, they who fittingly
        Should bear this burden which you bear, like maidens
        Keep house at home, while in their stead you two
        Are toiling to relieve my miseries.
        One, from the time she left her nursery
        And grew to her full strength, in my train ever
        Wanders in wretchedness, an old man's leader,
        Through the wild forest often journeying
        Foodless and footsore, toiling painfully
        Often—in rain and the sun's sultriness,
        Holding the comforts of her life at home
        As nothing, to the tending of her sire.
        While you, my child, sallied out once before
        Bringing your father all the oracles
        That were delivered as concerning me,
        Without the Cadmeans' knowledge, and became
        My faithful watcher, when they banished me;
        And now again—what story are you come
        To tell your father? what dispatch, Ismene,
        Transported you from home? for you are come
        Not empty, at least; of that I am assured;
        Nor without bringing me some cause for fear.
ISMENE   What sufferings, my father, I endured,
        Seeking your lodging and abiding-place,
        I will pass over; for I do not care

To feel the pain twice over, in the travail,
And after, in the telling. But the ills
Now compassing your two unhappy sons—
These I have come to shew. For formerly
They were both eager that the sovereignty
Should pass to Creon, and the city, so,
Not be defiled; professing to regard
The inveterate perdition of the race,
Such as had fastened on your woeful house;
But now some God, and an infatuate mind,
Has caused an evil struggle to arise
Between that pair, thrice miserable, to seize
Upon the government and royal power.
And now the lad, the younger of the twain,
Is robbing Polynices of the throne,
Who is his elder, and has driven him forth
Out of his native land. He, taking flight
(As is the general rumour in our ears)
To Argos in the Vale, is gaining there
New comrades and connexions to his side,
Swearing that Argos either shall forthwith
Humble the glory of the Cadmeans' land,[9]
Or else, exalt it to the height of heaven.
Dear father, this is not a wordy tale;
'Tis dreadful fact; and at what point the Gods
Mean to take pity upon your woes, I know not.

ŒDIPUS   And did you hope already that the Gods
          Would have some care for my deliverance?
ISMENE   Yes, father, after this new oracle.
ŒDIPUS   What is it? What has been revealed, my child?
ISMENE   That you shall be by the inhabitants
          Sought to hereafter, for their safety's sake,
          Whether in life or death.
ŒDIPUS   But who could profit
          By such as I?
ISMENE   On you, 'tis said, their power
          Comes to depend.
ŒDIPUS   What, now my life is finished,
          Do I begin to live?

[9]Cadmus was the acknowledged founder of Thebes. The city's people, therefore, bear
his name.

ISMENE   'Tis the Gods, now,
        Uplift you, who destroyed you formerly.
ŒDIPUS   To fall when young, and be set up when old,
        Is poor exchange!
ISMENE   And on this errand know
        That Creon will be here, and that ere long.
ŒDIPUS   With what intent, my daughter? Construe me.
ISMENE   To lodge you in the parts near Cadmean soil,
        So they may have you in their power, but you
        Never set foot within its boundaries.
ŒDIPUS   How are they helped by my lying at their doors?
ISMENE   Your being buried inauspiciously
        Brings them disaster.
ŒDIPUS   Even without a God
        One might conclude so far.
ISMENE   Therefore they seek
        To attach you, near their land, where you may be
        No longer your own master.
ŒDIPUS   Do they mean
        To shroud me in the dust of Thebes?
ISMENE   Nay, father,
        Taint of a kinsman's blood forbids it you.
ŒDIPUS   Then they shall never get me in their power.
ISMENE   That will go hard with men of Thebes one day.
ŒDIPUS   How should that be, my child?
ISMENE   Through wrath of yours,
        When they approach your grave.
ŒDIPUS   Child—what you say—
        Whence did you hear it all?
ISMENE   From envoys sent
        To inquire at Delphi's shrine.
ŒDIPUS   Was Phœbus he
        Who hath said these things of me?
ISMENE   So they report
        Who came to Thebes.
ŒDIPUS   Did either of my sons
        Hear it?
ISMENE   Yes, both alike, and well they know it.
ŒDIPUS   And did the varlets, when they heard it, still
        Prefer their kingship to regard for me?
ISMENE   I grieve to hear the question; all the same,
        Such is my news.

ŒDIPUS   Then may the Gods not quench
          The fated strife betwixt them, and the end
          May it be for me to give them, of that battle
          On which they are set, levelling their spear-points now!
          So neither shall that one of them abide
          Who holds the sceptre now, and throne, nor he
          Who has departed ever more return:
          Who verily, when I who fathered them
          Was thrust out of the land so shamefully,
          Stayed not nor screened me; but between them I
          Was sent adrift, sentenced to banishment.
          "A favour," you may say, "the city then
          Granted me, as of course, at my desire";
          Nay truly! for upon that selfsame day
          When my brain boiled, and to be stoned and die
          Seemed sweetest, there was no one that stood up
          To help me to my craving; but long after,
          When all the trouble was no longer green,
          And I perceived my passion had outstripped
          The chastisement of my offences past,
          Then was it that this happened; then the city
          Violently drave me from the land, at last;
          While they, their father's offspring, in whose power
          It lay to help their father, would not do it,
          But I have had to wander, out and on,
          Thanks to the little word they would not say,
          In beggary and exile. And from these,
          Being maidens, all that nature lends to them,
          Both sustenance and safety by the way,
          Ay and familiar comfort, I receive;
          While they preferred to their own father thrones
          And sceptred rule and territorial sway.
          But me for an ally they shall not gain;
          Nor ever from their Cadmean monarchy
          Shall benefit flow to them; this I know,
          Hearing the oracle she brings me now,
          And minding, too, that ancient prophecy
          Of mine, by Phœbus brought to pass on me.
          So now let them send Creon after me,
          And every lusty catch-poll in their town;
          For, gentlemen, if in the train of these,
          The awful Powers who guard your village-ground,
          You shall decide to summon up your force

In my behalf, then will you, for this city,
Procure a mighty saviour, and entail
Troubles on those, who are my enemies.
1 CITIZEN   First, you have won our pity, Œdipus,
Both for yourself and for your daughters; next,
Seeing that beside this pleading you propose
Yourself, to be a saviour for our land,
I am disposed to give you some good counsel.
ŒDIPUS   Stand my friend, most kind sir; and I will do
All that you bid me.
1 CITIZEN   Come and institute
Rites of purgation to the deities
Whose ground you trespassed on, when you came hither.
ŒDIPUS   After what fashion, sirs? instruct me.
1 CITIZEN   First
Bring holy water from a running stream;
But let your hands be pure.
ŒDIPUS   And afterward,
When I have drawn the limpid wave?
1 CITIZEN   There stand
Bowls, of an artist's carving; garland thou
Their rims, and the two ear-handles.
ŒDIPUS   With twigs,
Or bits of wool, or how?
1 CITIZEN   With a lock of wool,
New-shorn, ta'en from a yeanling ewe.
ŒDIPUS   So be it.
And after, how am I to make an end?
1 CITIZEN   Turn to the region where the dawn begins,
And pour libations.
ŒDIPUS   From the vessels, there,
Of which you spake, am I to pour them?
1 CITIZEN   Yes,
From each of three, one; and the last bowl drain.
ŒDIPUS   This last—how must I fill it, for the rite?
Tell me this too.
1 CITIZEN   With honey and water; add
No drop of wine.
ŒDIPUS   And when the bosky soil
Has taken these?
1 CITIZEN   Strew thrice nine olive-boughs
On either hand; and offer up this prayer.
ŒDIPUS   Ay, that is of most moment. Let me hear it.

1 CITIZEN   That as we call them Favourers, they would deign
        With favouring breasts to accept the supplicant,
        And save him; pray yourself, or in your stead
        Some other, speaking in an undertone,
        Not so as to be heard. Then come away
        And do not look behind you. This performed,
        I will stand by you gladly; otherwise,
        O stranger, I should have my fears for you.
ŒDIPUS   Girls, do you hear these people of the place?
ANTIGONE   We hear them well. Tell us what we must do.
ŒDIPUS   I cannot go; for neither have I strength
        Nor eyesight for the work—two hindrances;
        One of you two go and discharge this duty;
        For I suppose one spirit will suffice
        For tens of thousands, with good will, to do it.
        Make haste and set about it, anyhow;
        But do not leave me by myself alone;
        For in my frame there is not strength enough
        To creep unaided, or without a guide.
ISMENE   Well, I will go and do it. But the place—
        I want to know where I must look for it.
1 CITIZEN   Lady, beyond this thicket. Anything
        That you may need, there is one dwelling there
        Who will inform you.
ISMENE   I will betake me to it.
        Guard you our father here, Antigone.
        We may not take account of labour, even
        If we do labour, in a parent's cause.   [*Exit.*

I. 1.

1 CITIZEN   Stranger! 'Tis cruel to awake again
        The long since deadened pain;
        And yet I fain would learn—
ŒDIPUS   What is it, friend?
1 CITIZEN   The story of all that self-disclosed distress—
        Pitiful, remediless—
        Wherewith it was thy fortune to contend.
ŒDIPUS   Nay do not, for your hospitality,
        Open my ruthless wounds!
1 CITIZEN   I long to know,
        And to know right, that which is noised of thee
        So widely, and so unremittingly.

ŒDIPUS   Woe's me!
1 CITIZEN   Bear with me, I pray thee.
ŒDIPUS   Woe, ah woe!
1 CITIZEN   Hearken to my request;
         For I too hearken in all, at thy behest.

I. 2.

ŒDIPUS   Guilt overwhelmed me, friends—whelmed me, in sooth,
         (God be my witness!) undesigned, unsought;
         Nought was of purpose in the ills I wrought.
1 CITIZEN   To what effect?
ŒDIPUS   The city bound the chain
         Of an unhappy nuptial-bond on me,
         That knew not what I did.
1 CITIZEN   Didst thou in truth,
         As I hear said,
         Share an ill-omened bed
         With her—who was thy mother?
ŒDIPUS   O, I die,
         Stranger, to hear it uttered! And these twain—
1 CITIZEN   How say'st thou?
ŒDIPUS   Young
         Daughters of mine, twin curses!
1 CITIZEN   God!
ŒDIPUS   Are sprung
         From the same mother's travail-pangs, as I.

II. 1.

1 CITIZEN   Are these thy off-spring?
ŒDIPUS   Yes,
         And their sire's sisters also.
1 CITIZEN   Alas!
ŒDIPUS   Alas,
         Wave upon wave of evils, numberless!
1 CITIZEN   Thou didst endure—
ŒDIPUS   I endured misery;
         Yea, it abides with me.
1 CITIZEN   Thou didst commit—
ŒDIPUS   Nay, I committed nothing!
1 CITIZEN   How was that?
ŒDIPUS   I but received a boon, wretch that I was!

Such, that my service never merited at
The city's hands, to have the gift of it.

II. 2.

1 CITIZEN   How then, unhappy one? Wert thou the cause—
ŒDIPUS   What next? What wouldst thou know?
1 CITIZEN   Of thine own father's murder?
ŒDIPUS   O my heart!
  Thou hast struck me a second blow,
  Smart upon smart!
1 CITIZEN   Didst thou kill—
ŒDIPUS   Yea, I killed him. But the deed
  Had something in it—
1 CITIZEN   What is there to plead?
ŒDIPUS   Appealing to the laws.
1 CITIZEN   How could that be?
ŒDIPUS   I will declare to thee;
  Those whom I slew would have been slayers of me;
  Whence legally stainless, and in innocence,
  I stumbled on the offence.
1 CITIZEN   Here is our master Theseus, Ægeus' son,
  Come, at thy word, to do thine errand here.

[*Enter* THESEUS.]

THESEUS   Many aforetime having brought to me
  The bloody story of thine eyes put out,
  O son of Laius, I was ware of thee;
  And now, from rumour as I came along,
  I am the more assured; for by thy garb
  And thine afflicted presence we perceive
  That thou art really he; and pitying thee,
  Thou forlorn Œdipus, I would enquire
  With what petition to the city or me
  Thou and thy hapless follower wait on us?
  Instruct me; for calamitous indeed
  Must be the case disclosed by thee, wherefrom
  I should start backward; who remember well
  How in my youth I was a wanderer,
  Even as thy self; and strove with perils no less
  In my own person, on a foreign soil,
  Than any on earth; wherefore no foreigner,

Such as now thou art, would I turn aside
From helping to deliver; knowing well
That I am human, and have no more share
In what to-morrow will afford, than thou.
ŒDIPUS   Theseus, thy nobleness—without much talking—
Hath so vouchsafed, that little is required
For me to say. For thou hast named for me
Both who I am, and from what father sprung,
And from what country coming; wherefore now
Nothing is left me, but to speak the thing
Which I have need of, and my say is said.
THESEUS   That very thing now tell, that I may know it.
ŒDIPUS   I come, meaning to give this sorry body
A gift to thee; not goodly to the eyesight;
But better is the gain to come of it
Than beauty.
THESEUS   But what gain do you suppose
Your coming brings?
ŒDIPUS   In due time you will know;
Not just at present.
THESEUS   At what period
Will the advantage of your gift be shewn?
ŒDIPUS   When I am dead, and you have buried me.
THESEUS   O, you are claiming life's last offices;
But all that lies between—either you forget,
Or prize at nothing.
ŒDIPUS   Yes, because in them
I have all the rest summed up.
THESEUS   Tiny indeed
Is this request you proffer!
ŒDIPUS   No; look to it;
The coming struggle is not—is not light.
THESEUS   Do you speak of your own offspring and of me?
ŒDIPUS   King, they would fain convey me thither.
THESEUS   Well,
If you are not unwilling—to stay banished
Were hardly for your honour.
ŒDIPUS   When I wished it,
They were the hindrance!
THESEUS   O insensate one,
Wrath is not fitting in adversity!
ŒDIPUS   When you have heard me, censure; but as yet
Spare me.

THESEUS   Say on; for inconsiderately
      It fits me not to speak.
ŒDIPUS   Theseus, I have suffered
      Wrongs upon wrongs, most cruel.
THESEUS   Do you mean
      The old misfortune of your birth?
ŒDIPUS   O no;
      There is no Greek who does not babble of that!
THESEUS   What is this sickness then, of which you ail,
      Sorer than human?
ŒDIPUS   Thus it stands with me;
      By my own offspring was I hunted forth
      Out of my country; and I never more
      Can, as a parricide, again return.
THESEUS   Then why should they desire to send for you,
      To make you live remote?
ŒDIPUS   The divine lips
      Leave them no choice.
THESEUS   What sort of detriment
      Are they afraid of, from the oracles?
ŒDIPUS   It is their destiny to be overthrown
      Here, in this land.
THESEUS   And how shall come about
      The bitter feeling between them and me?
ŒDIPUS   Dear son of Ægeus, to the Gods alone
      Belongs it never to be old or die,
      But all things else melt with all-powerful Time.
      Earth's might decays, the body's might decays,
      And belief dies, and disbelief grows greenly;
      And varying ever is the passing breath
      Either 'twixt friend and friend, or city and city.
      For to some now, and by and by to some,
      Their friendship's pleasantness is turned to gall,
      Ay, and again to friendship. So in Thebes,
      Though all be now smooth weather there toward you,
      Yet, as he goes, the multitudinous Time
      Gives birth to multitudinous nights and days,
      Wherein, at a mere word, shall Theban steel
      Sever your now harmonious hand-claspings!
      Then shall my sleeping and invisible clay,
      Cold in the ground, drink their warm life-blood—if
      Jove be still Jove, and Jove-born Phœbus true.

But since it is unpleasing to declare.
The words that sleep unuttered, suffer me
To stay as I began, making but good
The pledge you gave; and you shall never say
(So but the Gods do not prove false to me)
That you received, into this land of yours,
In Œdipus, a thankless habitant.

1 CITIZEN   The man, my Liege, has constantly averred
He will perform these and like offices
Unto our land.

THESEUS   Who is there would reject
The tender of goodwill from such as he,
To whom, indeed, the hearth of comradeship
With us is ever open? and besides,
He, coming as a suppliant to the Gods,
Pays no small tribute to the land, and me.
Mindful whereof, I never will repel
The favour that he proffers; nay, I will
Replant him in our country. And if here
'Tis pleasant to the stranger to abide,
I shall enjoin you to take care of him;
Or if it pleases him to go with me—
Why, Œdipus, I leave to you the word,
Which you will choose. Your pleasure shall be mine.

ŒDIPUS   O Zeus, shower blessings on such men as this!

THESEUS   Which is your fancy? To go home with me?

ŒDIPUS   If it were lawful. But the spot is here—

THESEUS   For you to do—what? for I shall not hinder.

ŒDIPUS   For me to vanquish those who have banished me—

THESEUS   You magnify the advantage of your presence.

ŒDIPUS   If what you say abides, and you perform.

THESEUS   Be easy about me; I shall not fail you.

ŒDIPUS   I will not swear you, like some caitiff!

THESEUS   Nay,
You would gain nothing more than my word gives you

ŒDIPUS   How will you do it?

THESEUS   What fear you specially?

ŒDIPUS   There will come those—

THESEUS   These will take care for them!

ŒDIPUS   Mind how you leave me—

THESEUS   Teach not me my duty!

ŒDIPUS   Needs must, who fears.

THESEUS   My spirit is not afraid.
ŒDIPUS   You do not know the threats—
THESEUS   I know that none
    Shall drag you from this place in spite of me.
    As for their threatenings—many are the threats
    In anger spoken often, but in vain;
    For when the reason has come home again,
    The threats are vanished. And for them, I know,
    Though they take heart to talk portentously
    Of carrying you away, yet it may happen
    The sea between us will be found full wide,
    And hardly navigable. I bid you, rather,
    Be of good cheer, apart from my resolve,
    Since Phœbus sent you hither; and, at least,
    Even in my absence, I am well assured
    My name will guard you from all injury.   [*Exit.*

Chorus

I. 1.

    Stranger, thou art come to rest
    Where the pasturing folds are best
    Of this land of goodly steeds,
    In Colonus' glistening meads,
    Where the clear-voiced nightingale
    Oftenest in green valley-glades
    Loves to hide her and bewail;
    Under wine-dark ivy shades,
    Or the leafy ways, untrod,
    Pierced by sun or tempest never,
    Myriad-fruited, of a God;
    Where in Bacchanalian trim
    Dionysus ranges ever
    With the Nymphs who fostered him;

I. 2.

    And with bloom each morning there
    Sky-bedewed, in clusters fair
    Without ceasing flourishes
    The narcissus, from of old
    Crown of mighty Goddesses,

And the crocus, rayed with gold;
Nor do sleepless fountains fail,
Wandering down Cephissus'[10] streams;
But with moisture pure return,
Quickening day by day the plains
In the bosom of the vale;
These nor choirs of Muses spurn,
Nor the Queen with golden reins,
Aphrodita, light-esteems.

II. 1.

Also there is a plant, self-sown,
Untrained, ungrafted—never known,
That I have heard, in Asian soil,
Or Pelops' mighty Dorian isle,
Which, terror of the spears of foes,
In this our land most largely grows—
Grey nurse of boyhood, the Olive-Leaf;
Plant neither youth nor veteran chief
Shall e'er destroy with violent hand;
For that the face of Jove above it,
An ever watching guardian, and
The azure-eyed Athana, love it.

II. 2.

And further, more than all, we boast
The great God's bounty, prized the most
Of honours by our Mother-state—
Fair sea, fleet steed, and fruitful strain.
O Cronos' son, Poseidon, King,
Thou givest her this praise to sing!
Thou didst for these highways create
The bit, the courser to refrain;
And thy good oar-blades, fashioned meet
For hands of rowers, with bounding motion
Follow the Nereids' hundred feet,
In marvellous dance, along the Ocean.

---

[10]*Cephissus*] The largest river in the region of Attica, where Athens was the principal
city.

ANTIGONE   O highest extolled of lands, it is for thee
      To illustrate, now, these glorious words of praise.
ŒDIPUS   What is there new, my daughter?
ANTIGONE   Here comes Creon
      To meet us, father, and not escort-less.
ŒDIPUS   Now let the bourn of safety stand revealed,
      Friendliest of seniors, on your part, for me!
1 CITIZEN   Courage, it is at hand. If we are old,
      The vigour of our country has not aged.

[*Enter* CREON, *attended.*]

CREON   Gentle inhabitants of this your land,
      I read it in your eyes, you have conceived
      Some sudden apprehension at my coming;
      But spare reproach, and have no fear of me.
      For with no forceful aim am I come hither,
      Being an old man, and knowing I am arrived
      Before a city of no meaner power
      Than any in Hellas;[11] rather, I am sent—
      Old as I am—for to persuade this man
      To come along with me to Theban soil,
      Not upon one man's errand, but enjoined
      By all the folk, since it has fallen to me,
      By kinship, to bewail most grievously
      Of our whole city his calamities.
      Now therefore, O thou luckless Œdipus,
      Listen to me, and turn thy footsteps home.
      All the whole Cadmean people call for thee,
      And rightly; and among them I the most;
      Who, if I be not basest of mankind,
      As much the most, old sir, grieve at thy troubles,
      Beholding thee in misery, far from home,
      And yet a wanderer always, tramping on,
      Indigent, leaning on one handmaiden,
      Who I—God help me! never had surmised
      Could fall to such a depth of ignominy
      As this unhappy one has fallen to,
      Thee and thy blindness tending evermore
      In habit of a beggar—at her age—
      Maiden as yet, but any passer's prey!

---

[11]*Hellas*] Greece.

What, is it shocking, the reproach I cast
On you, and on myself, (wretch that I am!)
And the whole house? Then by our fathers' Gods,
Since what is blazed abroad can not stay hidden,
Hearken to me, and hide it, Œdipus;
Consent to seek your city and father's roof;
Not without salutation to this town,
For she deserves it well; yet it were just
More worship should be paid to her at home,
Who was your foster-mother formerly.

ŒDIPUS   Thou aweless villain, ready to adduce
Specious invention of just argument
From every case, why this attempt on me?
Why do you seek to take me, a second time,
In such a snare as must torment me most
If I were in your power? For formerly,
When I was sick of my domestic ills,
When to avoid the land had charms for me,
You would not grant the favour I desired;
But when I was now sated of my frenzy,
And it was pleasant to wag on at home,
Straightway you thrust me forth! you cast me out!
Never a jot you cared for all this kinship!
And now once more, when you perceive this city
And all her sons in friendship at my side,
You try, with your soft cruel words, to part us!
And yet what charm lies in befriending men
Against their will? since if a man to you
Refused a favour, when you begged for it,
And would give nothing, and then afterwards,
When you were satisfied of your desire,
And all the grace was graceless, proffered it,
Would not the pleasure so received be vain?
Such are the offers which you make to me,
Good in pretence, but evil in the trial.
Yea, these shall hear how I will prove you base;
You are come to take me, yet not take me home,
But plant me in your confines, that your city
May come off free from harm, of this land's doing:
You shall not have it! This, though, you shall have;
My spirit for evil haunting evermore
About your land; and this my sons shall have,
As much of my domain as may suffice

For them to die in! Can I not discern
Better than you what is the case of Thebes?
Far better; having better oracles,
Phœbus, and Zeus himself, who is his sire.
But treacherous is the tongue you have brought hither,
And of sharp edges; and in using it
You shall take more to hurt you, than to heal.
But—for I know I make no way with you—
Go! and let us live here. Give us content,
We are well enough provided, as we are.

CREON   Do you think my game is lost, as to your matters,
In this discussion, rather—or your own?

ŒDIPUS   All that I care for is that you should fail
Either to persuade me, or these by-standers.

CREON   O wretched man, have you no growth of sense,
At last, to boast of? Do you hug reproach
To your old age?

ŒDIPUS   You are adroit in tongue;
But righteous know I none, who speaks fair speeches
Whate'er his cause.

CREON   To say what's seasonable,
And to say much, are different.

ŒDIPUS   You, no question,
Say—O how little—and that seasonable!

CREON   Not in the judgment of a mind like yours!

ŒDIPUS   Depart; for I will speak for these as well;
Do not come cruising, keeping watch on me,
Where I must dwell.

CREON   These I attest, not you;
But for the answer you will make your friends,
If I once catch you—

ŒDIPUS   Who can capture me
Against the will of my defenders?

CREON   Yea,
Capture apart, you will be vexed anon.

ŒDIPUS   What sort of act is there behind this menace?

CREON   Of your two daughters one I have just seized
And sent; and her I will take presently.

ŒDIPUS   O sorrow!

CREON   You will have more occasion to sing sorrow,
Immediately, for this!

ŒDIPUS   You have seized my daughter?

CREON   [*pointing to* ANTIGONE] Yes, and will seize her, soon!

ŒDIPUS   Ho, gentlemen!
    What will you do? Will you prove false to me?
    Will you not hunt the villain off your soil?
1 CITIZEN   Withdraw sir, straightway; for you deal not rightly
    In this; nor yet in what you did before.
CREON   [*to the attendants*] Now is your time; carry the girl away;
    By force, if she will not consent to go.
ANTIGONE   Unhappy, whither shall I fly? What help
    Of God or man shall I lay hold on?
1 CITIZEN   Sir,
    What are you doing?
CREON   I will not touch the man;
    Only this maiden, who belongs to me.
ŒDIPUS   You lords of Athens!
1 CITIZEN   Sir, you do not rightly!
CREON   I do.
1 CITIZEN   How rightly?
CREON   I carry off what is mine.
                           [*Seizes* ANTIGONE.

ŒDIPUS   Help, Athens!

Chorus

    What d'ye mean, sirrah stranger?
    Will you not leave hold?
    You will come, presently,
    To a trial of force!

CREON   Keep off!

Chorus

Not from you, till you desist.

CREON   I tell you, you will have to fight my city,
    If you do me a harm.
ŒDIPUS   Did I not say so?
1 CITIZEN   [*to the attendant*] Take your hands off that maiden
      instantly!
CREON   Keep your commands for those you rule!
1 CITIZEN   I tell you,
    Let go!
CREON   [*to the attendants*] And I tell you, to go your ways.

Chorus

Come on, here, come!
Come on, neighbours all!
The town is being spoiled—
Our town, by force of arms!
Come on, here, to me!

ANTIGONE   I am dragged away, unhappy! O sirs—sirs!
ŒDIPUS   Where are you, daughter?
ANTIGONE   Here, borne along perforce.
ŒDIPUS   Reach out your hands, my child!
ANTIGONE   I am not able.
CREON   Will you not take her on?

[*Exeunt attendants with* ANTIGONE.

ŒDIPUS   Wretch that I am!
CREON   At least you shall not any longer make
    Of these two crutches an excuse to roam;
    But since you choose to gain a victory
    At the expense of your own land, and friends,
    By whose commands, although myself am royal,
    I do these things, why take it! for in time
    You will find out, I know, that neither now
    Are you doing well to your own self, nor yet
    Did so before, crossing your friends, to indulge
    The frenzy, which is your perpetual bane.
1 CITIZEN   Hold there, sir stranger!
CREON   Touch me not, I say.
1 CITIZEN   If they are lost, I will hold fast to you!
CREON   You shall soon spare a weightier pledge to Thebes;
    For I will lay my hands not on them only.
1 CITIZEN   What will you turn to?
CREON   I will seize him too,
    And carry him off!
1 CITIZEN   You speak a perilous word.
CREON   I swear it shall be done forthwith.
1 CITIZEN   Unless
    The ruler of this country hinder you!
ŒDIPUS   O shameless voice! Would'st thou lay hands on me?
CREON   Silence, I say!
ŒDIPUS   Nay, may these Goddesses
    Leave me but breath enough to lay this curse
    On thee, thou monster! who hast torn away

No other than an eye—by force—from me,
Lost—like the eyes I lost before! For this,
May the all-seeing among Gods, the Sun,
Give to thyself, and to thy family,
Even such a life in thy old age as mine!
CREON   You natives of this country, mark you this?
ŒDIPUS   They mark us both, and understand that I,
Wronged by thy deeds, with words defend myself.
CREON   I will not check my fury; though alone,
And slow with age, I will arrest him here.
ŒDIPUS   Unhappy that I am!

Chorus

How swollen is the pride
You are come with hither,
If you think, sir stranger,
To accomplish this!

CREON   I think it.

Chorus

Not, so long as Athens stands!

CREON   In his own right a weak man overcomes
A strong one.
ŒDIPUS   Hear ye what he mutters?
1 CITIZEN   What
He never will perform, (Zeus be my witness!)
CREON   That Zeus may know; you cannot.
1 CITIZEN   Is not this
Violence?
CREON   Yea, violence! but ye must bear it!

[*Attacks* ŒDIPUS.

Chorus

Help, people all!
Help, lords of the land!
Come on quickly, come!
They pass here, indeed,
Beyond all the bounds!

[*Enter* THESEUS, *attended.*]

THESEUS   What cry was that? What is it? In what panic fear
                Did you stay me sacrificing at the altar here
                To the Sea-God your patron? Speak, tell me the need
                At which I have hurried hither, with less ease than speed.
ŒDIPUS   O dearest friend—for your accost I know—
                I have but now been miserably abused
                At this man's hands!
THESEUS   How? Who misused you? Speak!
ŒDIPUS   Creon here, whom you see, has torn away
                The one poor pair of children left to me!
THESEUS   How say you?
ŒDIPUS   You have heard how I am wronged.
THESEUS   Some servant go as quick as possible
                To the altars by, and make the people all—
                Horsemen and footmen—from the sacrifice
                Hurry, with loosened reins, to the chief points
                Where pathways meet by which the packmen come,
                Lest the girls pass, and I become a mock
                To this my guest, worsted by violence.
                Go, as I bid you, quickly;   [*Exit Guard.*
                                As for him,
                Were I as far in anger as he merits,
                I had not suffered him to pass unscathed
                Out of my hands; but now, with the same law
                Shall he be suited, which he brought with him—
                That, and no other—Sir! you shall not stir
                Out of this country more, till you have brought
                And set those maidens here, for all to see;
                Since you have wrought unworthily of me,
                And of your lineage, and of your own land,
                Who, entering on a state that cares for right,
                And decides nothing without precedent,
                Must set at nought our country's officers,
                And in this onslaught hale away by force
                And make a prize of anything you please;
                Deeming my city to be void of men,
                Or manned with slaves, and my own self worth nothing!
                And yet it was not Thebes taught you this baseness;
                Thebes is not used to nourish lawless men,
                Nor would approve you, if she heard of you
                Despoiling me, yea and the Gods, by force

Dragging away poor creatures—supplicants.
I, if I did intrude upon your land,
Even if I had a cause more just than any,
Never, without the country's ruler's leave,
Whoever he might be, should have been found
Haling and leading captive; but I know
How guest to host ought to comport himself.
But you disgrace a state, that deserved better—
Your own—by your own act; and your full years
Leave you at once devoid of sense, and old.
So said I once before, and I now tell you;
Except you want to be compelled to stay
Against your will, an alien, in this land,
Have the girls brought back hither instantly!
You hear me say it, and what I say, I mean.

1 CITIZEN   Do you see the pass you have arrived at, Sir?
How you seem honest by your parentage,
And are found doing deeds iniquitous?

CREON   Not for that I account this city void
Of counsel or of manhood, as thou sayest,
O son of Ægeus, have I done this thing;
But apprehending no enthusiasm
About my kindred could have fallen on these,
That they, against my will, should cherish them;
And I felt certain they would not receive
A man polluted, and a parricide,
Nor one with whom was found the consciousness
Of an incestuous wedlock; such a Hill
Of Ares, rich in counsel, I well knew
To be established in this land of theirs,
That suffers not such vagabonds to dwell
Within their city's bounds; and in that trust
I undertook to make this capture mine.
And even this I should not have essayed,
But for the bitter curse by him denounced
On me, and on my race; for which, being wronged,
This, in return, I judged it right to do.
For of resentment there is no old age,
Other than death. No fret can reach the dead.
Now, you will do just what you please; for me—
Me friendlessness makes insignificant,
Although my words are just; yet when assailed,
Old as I am, I will attempt revenge.

ŒDIPUS   O front of impudence! Which thinkest thou
          Now to defile—My grey hairs, or thine own?
          Who hast spit forth out of thy mouth at me
          Murders and marriages and accidents,
          Which to my grief, not of free will, I suffered;
          Such was the will of Heaven, that had some cause
          For wrath, it may be, with our house, of old.
          Since for myself, I know you cannot find
          Any reproach of wrongfulness in me,
          That could have doomed me to commit these wrongs
          Against myself and mine; for, answer me,
          If to my father by an oracle
          The revelation came that he should die
          By his son's hands, how can you justly tax
          Me with the fact, whom neither father yet
          Then had begot, or mother had conceived,
          Me, who as yet had not begun to be?
          And if thereafter proving—as I proved—
          Hapless, I did lay hands upon my sire
          And slay him, nowise knowing what I did,
          Nor yet to whom I did it, how, I ask,
          Can you with reason blame the unconscious deed!
          And for my mother—are you not ashamed,
          O miserable! at forcing me to name
          Her marriage, your own sister's—as I will—
          I will not now be silent, you being grown
          To such a monster of outspokenness!
          She bare—ah yes, unknowingly she bare
          Me—who not knew! Woe worth the while to me!
          And having given me birth, she brought me forth
          Children—her own reproach! But of set purpose,
          For one thing, well I know, you spit this venom
          On her, and me; whereas I wedded her
          Unwitting, and unwillingly speak of it.
          But not for this my marriage, nor for that—
          That parricide, which you continually
          Throw in my teeth, bitterly upbraiding it,
          Do I consent to be called infamous.
          For answer me a question; but this one;
          If any person here upon the spot
          Drew near to kill you—you the just one—whether
          Would you enquire if he that sought your life
          Were your own father, or requite him straight?

You would requite the offender, I conceive,
If you love life; not look about for law.
Just such was the misfortune I incurred,
Led by the hand of Heaven; for which, I fancy,
Not even my father's spirit, were he alive,
Could say one word against me. And yet you—
(For just you are not, but think well to utter
All things, both lawful and unlawful,) you
Slander me with these sayings before them all!
Yea, you make free to fawn on Theseus' name,
And upon Athens—how decorously
She hath been ordered; and so lauding her,
You miss out this, that if there be a land
That knows what reverence to the Gods is due,
'Tis she herein excels, whence to remove
Me, the old suppliant, you assail my person,
And seize my daughters, and make off with them.
Wherefore these maiden Powers I invoke
With supplications, and with prayers adjure
To come, as aiders and auxiliaries;
So you may learn what sort of men they are,
By whom this city is defended.

1 CITIZEN   Sir,
The stranger is a good man; and his woes
Are horrible, and worthy of relief.

THESEUS   Enough of words; they speed, who have done the wrong,
While we, of the injured party, stand here still.

CREON   What is it you bid a poor weak man to do?

THESEUS   To shew the way, and to take me along,
That, if you have these maidens, whom we seek,
Inside our bounds, yourself may find them for me;
But if your guards are making off with them,
We need not toil; for there are others there,
No laggards, whom they never shall evade,
Crossing our frontiers, to give thanks to Heaven.
Lead forward! Know, sir captor, you are caught!
Fortune has trapped you, hunter! So it is,
Nothing abides of what is got by guile.
And you shall have no help; I am sure you have come
Not single, nor unfurnished, to the point
Of violence, such as you have here essayed,
But there was some one whom you trusted in.
I must look to it; I must not let this city

Be feebler than a single mortal's arm.
Do you take my sense? Or does my speaking seem
As idle, now, as when you framed this project?
CREON   Being here, you may say on, I shall not cavil;
But once at home, I shall know my part, too.
THESEUS   Ay, threaten us, and so—march! You, Œdipus,
Abide securely here; and credit me,
Till I have given your children to your arms,
Except I shall die first, I will not leave it.
ŒDIPUS   God speed you, Theseus, for your nobleness,
And for your duteous providence towards me.

[*Exeunt* THESEUS, CREON *and Guards.*

Chorus

I. 1.

I wish that I could be
Where foes are gathering fast,
Soon to be hurled together, brand on brand,
With clamour of battle! along either strand—
Pythian, or that where by the torches' light
Sit Queens, dispensing many a holy rite
To worshipping mortals on whose lips hath passed,
In mystic ritual, the golden key
Borne by their ministering Eumolpidæ;[12]
Soon, methinks, there
Shall Theseus, the awakener of the fight,
And that unconquered virgin pair,
Amid the fields hard by,
Join voices in one loud effectual rescue-cry!

I. 2.

Or haply pass they now
Out from the Œatid meads,
Nigh to that snow-clad mountain's western brow,
Flying on fleet steeds
Or swift contending chariots? He shall fail!
The battle spirit of our Athenian race
Is terrible; terrible in pride of place

[12]*Eumolpidæ*] Priests.

Are Theseus' children; lo where brightly shines
Curb beyond curb, and all along the lines
Of bridle-piece on bridle-piece of mail
      Come charging on
Horsemen on horses, warriors who revere
Athana, her to whom the horse is dear,
And him, the Sea-God, the land's guardian, Rhea's own son![13]

II. 1.

Are they at work? Do they linger yet?
    How I court the thought I shall greet, ere long,
Those maids much injured—the maids who met
    From kindred hands injurious wrong.
Zeus works—he is working a thing to-day;
    Prophet am I of a well-won field;
O would that I were as a storm-winged dove,
Swift and sure, on a cloud above
To soar to Heaven, and so survey
    The arms that triumph, the arms that yield!

II. 2.

Hail, great Master of Gods in heaven,
    All-seeing Zeus! With conquering might
To the chiefs of our land by Thee be it given
    To obtain this prize—to achieve this fight!
So Pallas Athana, thy awful maid,
    Grant it! Phœbus, too, I invoke,
The Hunter-God—come, visit us here,
With the chaser of dappled swift-footed deer,[14]
Thy sister—come, bring aid upon aid
    To this our country and these our folk!

1 CITIZEN   You will not say, sir wanderer, to your seer,
    He is no sayer of sooth; for I perceive
    Those girls conducted hither back again.
ŒDIPUS   Where? where? How say you?—What was that you said?

---

[13]*Rhea*] Titan, wife of Cronus, mother of Poseidon, Hera, Pluto, Ceres, and Hestia.
[14]The reference is to Artemis, goddess of the hunt and Apollo's sister.

[*Enter* THESEUS, ANTIGONE, ISMENE *and Guards.*]

ANTIGONE   O father, father, might some Deity
    Give you to look upon this best of men,
    Who brings us back to you!
ŒDIPUS   Child, are you there,
    You and your sister?
ANTIGONE   Yes; for Theseus' hands
    And his good followers', here, redeemed us.
ŒDIPUS   Come,
    My girl—Come to your father, both of you,
    And let me clasp your form—as I despaired
    Ever should be!
ANTIGONE   Have what you ask—the leave,
    Not without longing.
ŒDIPUS   Where—where are you?
ANTIGONE   Here,
    Both of us, coming close.
ŒDIPUS   My darling sprays!
ANTIGONE   O ay, dear to the stem!
ŒDIPUS   Props of my frame!
ANTIGONE   Poor hapless props, of a poor frame indeed!
ŒDIPUS   I have my darlings! Now I could even die
    Not all unhappy, these being by my side.
    Daughters, support me—one on either hand—
    Growing to the plant, from which you took your growth,
    So shall you end this wretched groping—lonely
    Until you came; then tell me, in fewest words,
    All that has happened; tender maids like you
    Need not to make long speeches.
ANTIGONE   Father dear,
    This is the man who rescued us; to him
    You must give ear; his is the deed; my part
    Will be full brief.
ŒDIPUS   O Sir, be not amazed,
    If seeing my children here, out of all hope,
    Makes me prolong discourse to weariness.
    For well I know, this kindness, joy to me,
    No other than yourself has shewn towards them.
    For you, and no man else, delivered them;
    And may the Gods bestow as I desire
    On you, and on this land; since among you
    Alone of men did I find piety,

And gentle dealing, and all truthfulness.
I know it, and these thanks are my return;
For what I have, I have, only through you.
And now, O king, stretch out your hand to me,
For me to touch, and kiss, if kiss I may,
That forehead. Yet—what am I babbling! How
Can I desire that you should touch a man—
Wretch that I am! to whom what taint of ills
Cleaves not? I cannot; nor will suffer you;
Only the man who has experienced it
Can sympathize with misery such as mine.
There, where you stand, I greet you; and henceforth
Be duly mindful of me, as to-day.

THESEUS   That in the pleasure these your children bring
You set wide bounds to your discourse of it,
That you preferred their converse in my room,
I have not felt amazement; no annoy
Possesses me, for this; I do not care
To have my life made glorious with fine speeches,
Rather than by my actions. And I shew it;
Seeing I have failed in nought of what I sware,
Old man, to you; for here they are with me,
Alive, unharmed of what was threatened them.
And now, what need to make a bootless boast
Of how the field was won? things which yourself
Will come to know from these, having them with you;
But on a matter I have met withal
In coming here just now, advise with me;
Since, though it seems a trifle, it is strange;
And it behoves us to make light of nothing.

ŒDIPUS   What is it, son of Ægeus? Tell me; I
Know nothing of the things you hint.

THESEUS   They say
A man, who is no countryman of yours,
And yet akin, has come and seated him
Before our altar of Poseidon here,
Where I was offering, when you summoned me.

ŒDIPUS   What countryman? What is it that he seeks
In taking sanctuary?

THESEUS   I do not know;
Save only that with you, as I am told,
He asks for a few words, an easy boon.

ŒDIPUS   But of what kind? This is no sanctuary
Taken for a trifling matter.

THESEUS   As they say,
    The object of his journey is to come
    To speech of you; then to depart, in safety,
    The way he came.
ŒDIPUS   Who can it be, that seats him
    As suppliant thus?
THESEUS   Think if you have some kinsman
    In Argos, who might seek this boon of you.
ŒDIPUS   O best of friends, stop, say no more!
THESEUS   What ails you?
ŒDIPUS   Do not request me—
THESEUS   To what purport, say?
ŒDIPUS   I know full well who is the supplicant,
    When I hear this.
THESEUS   Who can it be, with whom
    I am to have a quarrel?
ŒDIPUS   O king, my son;
    My abhorred son, whose words of all men's else
    Most grievously could I endure to hear.
THESEUS   But why? Can you not listen, and still not do
    What you mislike? How is the hearing pain?
ŒDIPUS   Most alien to a father's ears, sir king,
    Has that voice grown; do not put stress on me
    To yield in this.
THESEUS   Look if the sanctuary
    Does not compel it; whether a regard
    Must not be paid towards the God.
ANTIGONE   My father,
    Hearken to me, young though I am who speak.
    Suffer this friend to gratify the God
    And his own heart, in that which he desires;
    And grant it us, to let our brother come.
    Take heart! You cannot be seduced, perforce,
    From your resolve, by words that grate on you;
    But where's the harm of hearing? By discourse
    Are deeds, maliciously designed, bewrayed.
    You gave him being; then, if he did to you
    The wickedest and worst of injuries,
    Not even so, dear father, were it right
    For you to do him evil in return.
    O let him come! Others have bad sons too,
    And keen resentments; but, on being advised,
    They are charmed in spirit by the spells of friends.

Look to the past, not to the present; all
That you endured through mother and through sire;
If you regard it, you will find, I know,
That harmful passion ends in further harm.
You have reminders of it far from slight,
Maimed of your sightless eyes. Let us prevail!
It is not right that they whose prayers are just
Should play the beggar; nor that you yourself,
Who are being kindly treated, should not know
How to requite the kindness you receive.

ŒDIPUS   Child, I am conquered, by your words and his;
Your pleasure is my pain; be it as you please;
Only, if he you speak of shall come hither—
Sir host—never let any one get power
Over my life!

THESEUS   Twice to be told such things
I do not need; once is enough, old man;
Nor would I boast; yet be sure, safe you are,
If any of the Gods takes care of me.

[*Exit* THESEUS, *attended.*

Chorus

I.

Whoso thinks average years a paltry thing,
        Choosing prolonged old age,
He, to my mind, will be found treasuring
        A foolish heritage.
For when a man hath given him to fulfil
        What length of days he will,
Then many things are dealt him, in long days,
        That border hard on pain,
And things that please are hidden from the gaze;
    And when the doom of Hades is made plain,
Whereto belongs no bridal, and no quire,
        Nor any sound of lyre,
            Death, at the end,
        Waits, an impartial friend.

II.

Never to have been born is much the best;
        And the next best, by far,

To return thence, by the way speediest,
    Where our beginnings are.
While Youth is here, with folly in his train,
    (So full of cares our lot,)
Whose feet can fare beyond the reach of pain?
    What pains beset them not?
Murders, seditions, battles, envy, strife;
  Yea and old age, in hateful friendlessness,
This is our portion at the close of life,
    Strengthless—companionless;
      Wherewith abide
     Ills passing all beside.

Such are the aged; such am I;
    But he, this man of woes,
  Is beaten down on every hand,
  Like to some wintry Northern strand,
    Vext by the Ocean's blows;
Such waves of ill, so fell and high,
    Smite him, without repose;
Some from the settings of the Day,
    Some from his rising light,
Some on the midmost noontide ray,
    Some from the Alps of Night.

ANTIGONE   And here we have the stranger, I suppose—
    Nay, father, unattended—coming up
    This way; his eyes are wet with streaming tears.
ŒDIPUS   Who is the man?
ANTIGONE   The same whom all along
    We guessed at, Polynices. He is here.

[*Enter* POLYNICES.]

POLYNICES   Alack, what shall I do, girls? Must I first
    Mourn my own ills, or this my aged sire's,
    Beholding him? Whom I have met withal
    Outcast with you, here, on a foreign soil,
    Clad in a garb, whose horrid grime antique
    Has grown to suit with his antiquity,
    Marring his frame, while on the breeze his hair
    Streams from his eye-abated front uncombed,
    And, as it seems, akin to these, he bears

The scrip, for his poor belly's provender!
The which I recreant all too late perceive,
And do confess I am proved the worst of men
By your condition. Ask what I have done
Of none but me. But seeing how Clemency,
Even by the side of Zeus, sharing his throne,
Rules, in all acts, so let her find a place,
Father, with you; for remedies, indeed,
Still may remain, of what has been amiss,
But aggravations none.—Why are you silent?
Father, say something! Do not turn away!
Will you return me not an answer back?
Insult me with a dumb dismissal? Tell
Not even why you are enraged with me?
O offspring of this man, sisters of mine,
Try you to move our father's countenance,
Inexorable, unapproachable,
Not to dismiss me, the God's worshipper,
Thus in disgrace, answering me never a word!

ANTIGONE   Unhappy brother, what you come to seek
Tell us yourself; for out of many words,
Stirring delight, or breathing pity, or pain,
Come, to the voiceless, powers of utterance.

POLYNICES   I will speak out; for you direct me well;
First calling to my aid the God himself,
Up from whose shrine the sovereign of this land
Raised me, and sent me hither, promising me
Audience and answer and safe conduct hence.
The which I shall expect to meet with, sirs,
From you, from these my sisters, and my sire.
Next, I would tell you, father, why I came.
I have been driven out of my native land,
Because I claimed, being of an elder birth,
To seat me upon your imperial throne;
For which Eteocles, though my junior born,
Not overthrowing me in argument,
Nor coming to the test of arms or act,
But tampering with the people, exiled me.
Whereof the cause, above all else, I say,
Is your Erinys; and from soothsayers,
Moreover, so I hear. For when I came
To Argos of the Dorians, I obtained
The daughter of Adrastus to my wife,

And made confederates along with me
As many of the land of Apia
As are deemed first, and have been best approved
In war; meaning to gather against Thebes
My host of the Seven Lances in their train,
And either die upon the field, or else
Banish the authors of my banishment.
So be it! Then, why am I come hither now?
Father, with expiatory prayers to you,
Both for myself and my allies, who now
In seven arrays under seven pennons stand
All round the plain of Thebes. Among them comes
Amphiaraus the strong spearman, first
In war, first in the acts of augury;
The second is Ætolian, Œneus' son,
Tydeus; a third Eteoclus, Argive-born;
Talaus his father sends Hippomedon
Fourth; and the fifth, Capaneus, vaunts himself
That he will set the castle of Thebes on fire
And burn it to the ground; the sixth springs forward,
Parthenopæus the Arcadian, named
As being born of mother theretofore
Long time untamed, the trusty progeny
Of Atalanta; and your own son I—
(Or if disowned, then by ill destiny
Begotten, but at least called yours), I lead
The undaunted host of Argos against Thebes.
And all together for these children's sake,
Father, beseech you, and by your own life,
Praying you relax your heavy wrath at me,
Now marching to avenge me of that brother
Who thrust me forth, spoiled of my father-land.
For if there is a truth in oracles,
They say success is to the side you choose.
Wherefore I implore you, by the water-springs—
Yea by the Gods of Thebes, hearken and yield;
For I am poor and exiled; so are you;
And under the same lot both you and I
Cringe to a stranger for a lodging. He
Meanwhile, at home, a monarch, well a day!
Lives delicately, and derides us both;
But with short effort, after small delay,
If you cooperate with my design,

       Him will I shatter! and so take you home,
       And in your own house place you, and myself,
       And cast him out by force. With your goodwill
       I may indulge this boast; but, without you,
       I must lack strength even to come off with life.
1 CITIZEN Now for his sake who sent him, Œdipus,
       Say what is meet, and send the man away.
ŒDIPUS   Sirs, wardens of this country—were not he
       Theseus, who sped him on his way to me,
       Deeming it fitting I should answer him,
       He never should have heard my voice at all!
       But now, being so far graced, he shall depart
       With that within his ears shall sober him
       All his life long. O most desertless villain,
       Who, when you held the sceptre and the throne
       Which now your brother has achieved in Thebes,
       Yourself expelled me—your own father—me
       Made homeless—drove to wear this livery,
       Which you shed tears to see, now you have come
       To walk in the same evil straits with me!
       This is no stuff to weep for; rather is it
       For me to bear, mindful, howe'er I live,
       That you are my destroyer. For you made me
       Familiar with this woe; you exiled me;
       And by your act made vagabond, I beg
       My daily bread from others. Had I not
       Fathered these girls, to be my cherishers,
       I had been dead, for aught you did for me;
       But now these keep me, these my cherishers,
       These men, not women, for their ministering;
       And ye are sprung from others' loins, not mine,
       Wherefore Heaven frowns upon thee—yea, not yet
       As it soon shall frown, if these cohorts move
       Toward Theba's hold; for it may never be
       That thou shalt storm that city; rather, first,
       Thou, and thy brother as well, blood-stained, shalt fall.
       Such curses upon you I denounced before,
       And summon, now, to come and fight for me,
       And make you learn true filial reverence,
       And cease your scorn, although the sire be blind,
       Who fathered sons like you! These did not so.
       Therefore thy supplication and thy throne
       Fall 'neath its sway, if Justice as of old

Sits equal in the ancient rule of Jove.
Hence! I disown thee, reptile! of base souls
Basest! and take with thee this doom of mine,
Never to win thy native land in fight,
Nor to return to Argos in the Vale,
But by a kindred hand thyself to fall,
Him having slain, who was thy banisher.
This is my curse! And to the abyss I call,
Hated, of Hades, where my father is,
To be thy place of exile; and I call
These Powers, and Ares, who in both of you
Hath sown this monstrous hate. Hear me, and go;
And as you go, tell all the Cadmeans,
Ay, and your trusty allies, what recompense
Is to his own sons dealt, by Œdipus.

1 CITIZEN   I am sorry, Polynices, for the errand
On which you came; now get you back with speed.

POLYNICES   Woe for my journey, woe for my mischance,
Woe for my comrades! To an end like this
Did we set out from Argos on our way!
Such as it is impossible to tell
To any of my fellows, or to turn
Their footsteps backward; only this is left,
Silent, to meet my fate. O misery!
Sisters of mine, his daughters! You have heard
The hard words of our father, cursing me;
I charge you in Heaven's name, if that father's curse
Shall be fulfilled, and a return for you
Be granted home, do not you look on me
With contumely, but lay me in my tomb,
And grant me funeral rites. Then on that praise
Which from your labour for your father's sake
You now derive, shall rise a second praise,
As ample, through your ministering to me.

ANTIGONE   Polynices, I entreat you, yield to me!

POLYNICES   Tell me in what, dearest Antigone!

ANTIGONE   March back at once to Argos! Do not ruin
Yourself—and Thebes!

POLYNICES   That is impossible;
How could I lead the selfsame army forth,
If I had faltered once?

ANTIGONE   But why again
Must you get angry, boy? Where is your profit

In overthrowing your country?
POLYNICES   To be banished
    Is a dishonour; and for me, the elder,
    To be so flouted by my brother.
ANTIGONE   Then
    Do you not see that you are carrying out
    His prophecies forthright, who spells you death,
    Each from the other's hand?
POLYNICES   He wishes it.
    No, no retreat is left us.
ANTIGONE   Woe for me!
    But who that heard the things he prophesied
    Will dare to follow?
POLYNICES   Nay, we will tell no tales.
    It is the merit of a general
    To impart good news, and to conceal the bad.
ANTIGONE   Is this the course you have resolved on, boy?
POLYNICES   Ay—stay me not. Now to this course of mine
    Must I give heed, luckless and evil made
    By him, my father, and his cleaving curse.
    But as for you, God speed you, as you do
    My hest in death—since you will have nought further
    To do for me in life. Unhand me now.
    Farewell. You will behold my face no more.
ANTIGONE   O woe is me!
POLYNICES   Do not lament for me.
ANTIGONE   Who but must mourn thee, brother, rushing thus
    On death foreseen?
POLYNICES   If needs must, die I will.
ANTIGONE   Not so, but hear me!
POLYNICES   Ask not what may not be.
ANTIGONE   Unhappy that I am, if I lose thee!
POLYNICES   This is in Destiny's hands, or thus to be,
    Or not to be. For you—the Gods I pray
    You never meet with ill; for you deserve,
    All will confess, not to be miserable.   [*Exit.*

Chorus

I. 1.

    Here are new griefs, new and calamitous,
    From sources new, made manifest to us,

           Of the blind stranger's making;
           Except, indeed, his fate is overtaking:
    For of no doom from Heaven can I declare 'tis vain.
           The end Time sees, yea, sees alway;
           Time, that o'erthrows to-day,
    Time, that with morning's light uprears again.   [*Thunder.*

1 CITIZEN   Heavens! how it thundered!
ŒDIPUS   Children, my children! will some bystander
    Fetch the most excellent Theseus hither?
ANTIGONE   Father,
    What is the end for which you summon him?
ŒDIPUS   This thunder, winged by Jove, must carry me
    Straightway to Hades. Send at once, I say.   [*Thunder.*

Chorus

I. 2.

Hark with what might the unutterable roar
Of Jove's own bolt comes crashing down once more!
    The very hair on my head
    Stands up for dread;
My spirit quails.—There flames lightning from Heaven again!
    What will the issue be?
    I tremble at it: for surely not in vain
Is it sent forth—never innocuously.

                           [*Loud thunder.*

1 CITIZEN   You mighty Heavens! Thou Jove!
ŒDIPUS   Daughter, the appointed ending of my life
    Has found me, and may not be averted more.
ANTIGONE   How do you know it? By what conjecture comes
    This certainty?
ŒDIPUS   I feel it. With all speed
    Let some one go and fetch this country's king.   [*Thunder.*

Chorus

II. 1.

Hark again, hark,
    The echoing clap resounds on either hand.

Have mercy, O God, have mercy, if aught of dark
   Thou art now bringing to our mother-land!
     May he bring luck who meets me!
     Nor, now the man who greets me
  Is fraught with doom, let it be mine to share
A fruitless boon—King, Jove, to thee I make my prayer!

ŒDIPUS   Is the man nigh, my children? Will he come
   While I still live, and reason rules my mind?
ANTIGONE   What is the trust, which in your mind you crave
   To breathe in Theseus' ears?
ŒDIPUS   To pay to him,
   For good he did me, a complete return,
   Such as I promised in receiving it.

Chorus

II. 2.

   Hither, my son,
   Quick, quick—howbeit thine offerings are placed
High in the hollow of his altar-stone
   To the sea's lord, Poseidon, come with haste!
     Thee and thy city and friends
     The stranger-guest pretends
   To pay with profit, for his profiting,
In righteous measure. Hasten and come forth, our king!

[Enter THESEUS, *attended.]*

THESEUS   What is this general din, sounding anew,
   Loud from yourselves, and from the stranger plain?
   Is it that bolt from Jove, or shower of hail,
   Has burst upon you? Anything, while Heaven
   Is raising such a storm, is credible.
ŒDIPUS   King, thou art here at need; yea, and some God
   Has given thee good speed of this thy way.
THESEUS   What is the new event which has arisen,
   O son of Laius?
ŒDIPUS   End of life to me.
   And I am anxious not to die forsworn,
   In what I promised to this city and thee.
THESEUS   But under what death-symptom do you labour?

ŒDIPUS   The Gods are their own heralds, telling me,
      Belying nought of tokens fixed before.
THESEUS   How do you say that this is shewn you, sir?
ŒDIPUS   The frequent thunderings continuous,
      And frequent-flashing arrows, from the hand
      Invincible—
THESEUS   You move me; for I see
      You are a mighty soothsayer, and your words
      Do not come false. Say, then, what we must do.
ŒDIPUS   I will inform thee, son of Ægeus,
      Of what shall be in store for this thy city,
      Beyond the harm of time. Of my own self,
      Without a hand to guide me, presently
      I will explore a spot wherein, in death,
      I am to rest. Never to any man
      Say where 'tis hidden, or whereabouts it lies;
      So may it ever bring thee vigour, more
      Than many bucklers, or the hireling spear
      Of neighbours. But the place—a mystery
      Not to be put in language, thou thyself
      Shalt learn when thou goest thither, but alone;
      For not to any of these citizens,
      Nor to my daughters, though I love them well,
      Will I declare it. Keep it to thyself;
      And, when thou art coming to the end of life,
      Disclose it but to one, thy foremost; he
      To him who shall come after shewing it,
      For ever. So shalt thou inhabit still
      This city, unwasted by the earth-sprung seed;
      While swarms of towns, however men may live
      Good neighbours, lightly try to injure you.
      For the Gods mark it well, though they are slow,
      When any turn to folly, and forsake
      Their service; such experience, Ægeus' son,
      Do thou eschew; nay, what I preach, thou knowest.
      Now—to the place! The message from on high
      Urges me forth; let us not linger now.
      Here, follow me, my daughters! in my turn,
      Look, I am acting as a guide to you,
      As you were mine, your father's. Come along!—
      Nay, do not touch me; let me for myself
      Search out the hallowed grave where, in this soil,
      It is my fate to lie. Here, this way, come;

This way! for Hermes the Conductor and
The Nether Queen are this way leading me.
O Light—my Dark—once thou wast mine to see;
And now not ever shall my limbs again
Feel thee! Already I creep upon my way
To hide my last of life in Hades. Thou,
Dearest of friends—thy land—thy followers—all,
May you live happy; and in your happiness
Fortunate ever, think of me, your dead!

[*Exeunt* ŒDIPUS, THESEUS, ANTIGONE, ISMENE, *and attendants.*

Chorus

1.

If sound of my prayers may rise unto Her who is hid from sight,
If worship of mine may approach thee, the King of the shadows of
        night,
                Aïdoneus, Aïdoneus[15]—
                I entreat that this stranger
May pass right well, without sound of grief, by a painless doom,
To the hiding-place of the dead beneath, and the Stygian home.
—Though many are the sorrows that visit thee, many thy labours in
        vain,
It may be, a Power that is righteous intends to uplift thee again.

2.

Hail, Queens of the realms of Earth! All hail, the unconquered frame
Of the Hound,[16] that crouched, we were told, at the Gate whither all
        men came,
                And growled from its caverns,
                (So the story went ever,)
As Hades' champion and guard—whose steps, I pray, may be led
Far off, when the stranger comes to the nether fields of the dead!
—O Thou that art born of Earth, the begotten of the Deep,
Thee I invoke, the giver of unending sleep.

[*Enter a Messenger.*]

---

[15]*Aïdoneus*] Pluto, God of the Infernal Regions.
[16]*the Hound*] Cerberus, the multi-headed dog which guards the gates to the
   Underworld.

MESSENGER   Sirs, to cut short, as far as possible,
   What I would say—Œdipus is no more;
   But for what there befell, there are no words
   To tell it in brief space; nor was it brief,
   All that was done.
1 CITIZEN   Is the poor wanderer gone?
MESSENGER   Yes, he is quit of his life-trouble.
1 CITIZEN   How?
   Was't by some heaven-sent end—poor soul—and calm?
MESSENGER   Truly the event is meet to wonder at.
   First, in what fashion he set forth from hence,
   You must have seen, being present, even as I;
   None of his company conducting him,
   But he himself shewing to us all the way.
   Next, having reached the threshold of that chasm
   Whose root is in the Brazen Stairs below,
   There, upon one of the diverging paths,
   Nigh to the hollowed basin where are kept
   The tokens of the sure-abiding bond
   'Twixt Perithous and Theseus, he stood still;[17]
   Thence halfway to the stone from Thoricus,[18]
   Betwixt the hollow pear-tree and marble tomb,
   He sate him down; then doffed his grimy robe;
   And then, crying to his daughters, bade them bring
   Waters to wash, and pour, out of some stream;
   Which twain, proceeding to the opposing slope
   Of verdurous Demeter, with small delay
   Brought to their father that he sent them for;
   And him they washed, and decked in such attire
   As is in use; and when, now, nought remained
   Unsatisfied of all that he desired,
   Sounded from Hades thunder, and the maids,
   As they heard, shivered; and at their father's knees
   Fell down, and wept, beating their breasts, and raised
   Wailings prolonged, unceasing. He the while,
   Soon as he heard their bitter note of woe,
   Folding his arms about them, said; "For you,
   My girls, this day there is no father more;

[17] Perithous and Theseus together attempted to rescue Persephone from Hades, but they were unable to outdo Pluto.

[18] Thoricus was another hero of the region. His stone, the pear tree and the marble tomb are all presumed to have been sacred spots, ritual stopping points on the route to Hades.

For all things now are ended that were mine;
And now no longer need you bear for me
The burden of your hard tendance, hard indeed—
I know it, my children; but one single word
Cancels the evil of all cares like this;
Love, which ye had from no one more than me;
Of whom bereft, you for the time to come
Must live your life." So they all wept aloud,
Clinging to each other; but when they were come
To end of lamentation, and the cry
Rose up no longer, silence reigned awhile.
Then suddenly some voice shouted his name;
So that the hair of all stood up for fear;
For a God called him—called him many times,
From many sides at once: "Ho, Œdipus,
Thou Œdipus, why are we tarrying?
It is full long that thou art stayed for; come!"
He, when he felt Heaven summoned him, bespake
That the land's king, Theseus, should come to him;
And, when he came, said to him, "O dear friend,
Pledge me, in the ancient fashion, your right hand
To these my children, (and you, girls, give him yours,)
And swear—never to yield them willingly,
But as you purpose now to accomplish all
In kindness, ever, that is good for them."
He, of his gentleness, agreed; and sware,
(But not condoling,) to his guest, to do it.
And straightway as he sware it, Œdipus,
Touching with sightless hands his daughters, said:
"Now, children, you must leave this place; bear up
In spirit, as befits your nobleness;
Look not upon the sights you may not see,
List not the voices which you must not hear,
But with all speed depart; let but the king,
Theseus, be present, and behold the end."
While he thus spake, we hearkened, all of us;
Then followed we the maidens, grieving sore,
With streaming tears. When we had gone apart,
After short space we turned, and saw far off—
The man, indeed, nowhere still visible—
Only the king's self, holding up his hand
Over his face, so as to shade his eyes,
As if some sight of terror had appeared,

Awful, intolerable to gaze upon;
Then, in a moment, without interval,
We saw him kneel, worshipping Earth, and Heaven
The abode of Gods, both in one act, together.
But he—what death he died, save Theseus' self
There lives not any mortal who can tell.
For neither any fire-fraught thunderbolt
Rapt him, from Heaven, nor whirlwind from the sea
Stirred up to meet the moment; but some guide
Sent from above, or depth of the earth beneath
Opening to take him, friendly, without pain.
For not as of one mourned, or with disease
Grown pitiable, was his departure; but
If any ever was so, wonderful.
—If what I say seems folly, I can spare
The assent of those to whom I seem a fool.

1 CITIZEN   And where now are his daughters, and those friends
Who did attend them?

MESSENGER   They, at least, not far;
For sounds of wailing unmistakeable
Declare them to be moving up this way.

[*Enter* ANTIGONE *and* ISMENE.]

I. 1.

ANTIGONE   Alas, it is for us, it is for us to rue,
Not once alone, but evermore anew,
Unhappy that we are, the fatal strains
Of our sire's blood implanted in our veins.
      For whom, erewhile,
We ceaselessly endured a world of toil,
And have to tell, at last, of most unmeasured ill,
        Beheld and suffered, still.

1 CITIZEN   But what has happened?

ANTIGONE   You can guess it, friends.

1 CITIZEN   He is gone?

ANTIGONE   Yes, as one would most wish for him
      —What wonder? In whose way
      Nor war nor ocean lay,
But viewless regions rapt him home,
Sudden, by some mysterious doom,

While on our sight
The gloom of night,
Deathful and desolate, is come.
For how shall we sustain
Life's heavy load of toil,
Wandering o'er the billowy main,
Or on some foreign soil?
ISMENE   I know not. O that with my sire's last breath
I by some sudden death
Might perish! for the life that is to be
Seems worse than death to me.

Chorus

O children, worthiest pair, what heaven may send
Bear—to the end,
And let your grief be mild; the way by which you came
You have no cause to blame.

I. 2.

ANTIGONE   Even the ills of life, it may be, we regret.
For what indeed was no-wise charmful, yet
Became, to me, a life not without charms
The while I had my father in my arms.
O father dear,
Wrapped evermore in nether darkness drear,
O not for thine old age mightest thou ever be
Unloved by her and me!
1 CITIZEN   He fared—?
ANTIGONE   He fared even as he wished to do.
1 CITIZEN   How was it?
ANTIGONE   Upon that foreign soil he chose
Died he! For ever laid
Low, in the kindly shade,
He left behind no tearless grief,
No measured mourning, dull and brief,
These eyes are wet
With weeping yet,
Nor know I how to find relief.
Oh not for thy desire
In a strange land to die,

Need'st thou have perished, O my sire,
Thus, with no loved ones by!
ISMENE   O wretched that I am! What future fate
Me must await
And thee, my sister, lingering here alone,
And our dear father gone!

Chorus

But now he is at last thus happily
From life set free,
Cease this lamenting, friends! From evils, in some shape,
No mortal can escape.

II. 1.

ANTIGONE   Back let us haste, dear sister!
ISMENE   What to do?
ANTIGONE   A longing is upon me—
ISMENE   What?
ANTIGONE   To view
The earth-bound home—
ISMENE   Of whom?
ANTIGONE   Our father—woe is me!
ISMENE   But is it not forbid? Do you not see?
ANTIGONE   Why should it make you chide?
ISMENE   This too, that—
ANTIGONE   Well, what next?
ISMENE   Without a tomb,
Lonely, he died!
ANTIGONE   Take me to him, and slay me by his side!
ISMENE   Alas, unhappy, whither should I flee,
To live, once more, a life of misery,
In the old loneliness and poverty!

II. 2.

1 CITIZEN   Dear friends, fear nought!
ANTIGONE   Where should I shelter me?
1 CITIZEN   Truly there was a shelter, long ago—
ANTIGONE   How?
1 CITIZEN   For your fortunes, that they should be free

From evil destiny.
ANTIGONE   Nay, that I know.
1 CITIZEN   What is it, then, that doubles your concern?
ANTIGONE   'Tis that I know no way for our return
            To our own home.
1 CITIZEN   Care not to seek it!
ANTIGONE   I am overcome
            With weariness.
1 CITIZEN   Time was, you were so.
ANTIGONE   Yea,
            Sorely before, but now surpassingly.
1 CITIZEN   Truly it was yours to stem a stormy sea!
ANTIGONE   Whither, O Jove, shall we direct our way?
            Towards what point of hope—alas the day!
            Doth God impel me, and forbid my stay?

III.

[*Enter* THESEUS, *attended.*]

THESEUS   Children, cease to lament; for griefs, where
            Grace from the Nether Gods awaits us,
            Blessing all fortunes,
                Sorrow is causeless; nay, were sin.
ANTIGONE   O son of Ægeus, we are thy suppliants.
THESEUS   For what boon, my children?
ANTIGONE   We too
            Fain would look on our father's tomb.
THESEUS   Nay, the approach to it is forbidden us.
ANTIGONE   King, how say you, master of Athens?
THESEUS   He, my children, gave me commandment
            That no mortal's foot should trespass
            Near those precincts,
            Or give name to the ark of refuge
            Where he dwells; which things, he told me,
            Duly observing,
            I might evermore keep these confines
            Free from annoyance;
            And so Heaven o'erheard me swear it,
                And the omniscient Oath of Jove.
ANTIGONE   Well, if such be the way he willed it,
            Let that fully suffice. Now send us

Back to our ancient Thebes; it may be
We may ward off ruin, impendent
O'er our brethren.
THESEUS   I will do it at once, and all things
Such as I purpose, for your service,
And his pleasure, our dead, this moment
Rapt far from us; I may not tire.

Chorus

Cease, no longer upraise your wailing;
All these promises shall not fail.

[Exeunt.